THE GARDEN
AFTER THE RAIN

THE GARDEN AFTER THE RAIN

BEDTIME STORY AND ACTIVITY BOOK FOR CHILDREN 4-8 YEARS

Seema Johri

PARTRIDGE
A Penguin Random House Company

To order additional copies of this book, contact
Partridge India
000 800 10062 62
www.partridgepublishing.com/india
orders.india@partridgepublishing.com

CONTENTS

SOME FACTS

Telling Bed Time stories to our children, which are positive, must be done in each family. They do play a crucial role in overall growth and personality development of our tiny-tots. While caring Moms and Dads are full of good intentions, they find it hard to fit stories in their busy schedules. And surveys have found that 8 out of 10 parents believe that the children's attitude can be corrected by reading good Bed Time Stories.

By narrating stories to our little stars at night, we are not simply being physically close to them but emotionally too. Nothing can replace the feeling when our child is lying cuddled and hearing every word carefully that we have to say and tell. It is a unique opportunity for them to share some relaxed quality time with parents, away from the rush and stress of daily living. These quiet minutes each day become a precious moment for them and this extra attention makes them definitely feel secure in our love.

It is true that by telling Bed Time story we can actually improve children's motor skill. Many medical research studies have shown that this activity can actually enhance their speech and language development and the kids do better at school.

It is also a fact that instead of lecturing our children for the right and wrong, we can prepare them to take up challenges of different kinds by simply reading the stories at night. The children hear the basic idea contained in the story, try to predict events and improve their reasoning powers. They get ready for what choices they should make in life and enhance their skill on "Values".

Last but not least, telling Bed Time story is a fun ritual to relieve anxiety and insecurity of present day 'Today' and the children sleep much better at night thereafter.

1

The morning magic

*I*t was summer holidays for the children. Joshi family decided to take the three of them out for a walk each day, early in the morning.

The first day the children were excited. They got up early and got ready with their shoes on. They had good fun while trekking. All the way, they were laughing, picking up the flowers, kicking the pebbles and sometimes chasing each other, it was all fun.

"Hey! Where is Arnav?" mom asked suddenly.

Arnav was not there and no one knew from when.

"We must have lost him on the way and we must find him immediately," said a concerned Dad. A worried family looked everywhere but Arnav was not found.

And it so happened, that little Arnav was tired and he walked slower than the others. All of sudden, he noticed a huge banyan tree in a corner of the road with a very strange message, it said,

I am a magic tree, get some kick!

Use magic words and see the trick!!

The walk was boring and little Arnav wanted to enjoy so he tried all kinds of magical words that he knew to see the magic.

"Abra Ka Dabra!"

"Jai Hanuman!!"

"Khul Ja Sim Sim!!!" he shouted all, one by one.

But these were not the pass words and the magic tree did not respond to them. A desperate Arnav fell on the tree's root then and requested earnestly,

"Please tree, please help me, and give me some clue."

And, ... Lo, that was the right word, **'Please.'**

The trunk of the huge banyan opened like a door and what a sight it was!

_ It was 'Tree's Green Kingdom'.

Arnav entered the door slowly. There were flowers all around, a bit like 'Green' daisy, but so much bigger than the ones in Arnav's garden. And there were great big 'Green' fruits like cherry, strawberry, mango, plum and apricot.

The tree ate only honey and jam but he gave Arnav anything that he wanted— there were all sorts of green chocolates, green ice cream and green cakes.

All the tree's children danced and invited Arnav to join them. There was a choir of green canaries, green mynah and green cuckoos and they all whistled and cheeped in tune.

Eating and dancing, Arnav forgot all about his family and walk and the time flew fast. When he wanted to come out, one more board appeared before him that said,

Come to me, if you want more!

Use magic words, to go back home!!

Little Arnav knew now which word to speak. **'Thank you'** *He said nicely and came out.*

The worried Joshi family found Arnav fast asleep beneath a banyan tree and when they shook him up, he was **'Sorry'** *for spoiling their morning walk.*

2

Rati the doll

It was beginning of January in Varanasi and the winter was at its peak all around.

Inside her house, on a Sunday, little Tvisha was down with flu and fever. She was on a bed rest and not allowed to go out to play with her friends.

No wonder, she was feeling very bored!

Not so long ago, when Tvisha had just learnt to read and write, she was given a doll named Rati on her birthday. It was a beautiful soft toy made by her grandmother and was almost as big as her in size. Tvisha doted on her lovely doll and did all fun things together throughout the day. She also loved cuddling Rati at night to sleep. Every night, on her white board, Tvisha would write her daily activity and that consisted of her doll, Rati, only.

> **Mummy is busy, Daddy is away!**

> **Me and Rati, played hide and seek today!!** *And so on.*

Tvisha and Rati were inseparable those days.

Once Tvisha with her family had gone to Mumbai on a holiday and they had plans to see Ajanta Ellora, Gateway of India and so many other places. But Tvisha forgot Rati back home and without her, she was miserable. She kept awake the whole night and poor parents had to cancel their trip thereafter. Reaching home, Tvisha wrote on her board,

> **Holiday got wasted, it is pity!**

> **But life is no fun without Rati!!**

4

For months and months now, Tvisha had almost forgotten about Rati. She had been playing with her new friends: Aisha, Meethi and Ripu. And Rati, sitting in a corner of Tvisha's room did not like that at all. She would often remember the good old days when Tvisha carried her always around. They were so happy together.

In her room, a sick Tvisha could hear her friends playing outside; no-one had come to visit her.

"They must have forgotten about me," she cried when suddenly she saw Rati smiling at her lovingly.

Lo, Tvisha ran and hugged her like a lost friend.

Tvisha spent the rest of the day with Rati doing things that they did earlier. They played home-home, raced up and down the bed and watched the jet passing by their window together. Later, when Tvisha was tired she cuddled Rati close and went off to sleep. And before sleeping, she wrote in her diary,

It is cold, it is chill,

I have fever, I took some pill!

Rati is my friend, best still,

She gave me company when I was ill!

Rati was delighted, Tvisha loved her even now.

3

The sail boat

Ever since Priya won the first prize in the Inter School Drawing Competition, she had been on the top of the world.

Over the sea,

    And over the land,

My name would travel far away.

    Chasing, chasing my sweet dreams,

Not minutes and hours,

    I am all the day.

Priya sang this song often while creating something new and declared proudly to all her friends,

"You will see my name on a newspaper as the greatest artist of India one day."

Priya was forever boasting about her skill and her friends did not like this for long. Very few of them chose her company and even her best friend Shaina started ignoring her and made friends with Aditi instead.

For all her creativity, Priya was now a lonely girl.

Last year when Priya got admission in this school, she made friends quickly and an ever friendly Shaina became her best friend. Shaina lived close to her house and they both played together every evening, without fail. Sometimes they would quarrel and often they argued but then they would make up again. It was never a serious matter like this.

Priya complained to her mother about it and her mother advised her to be humble in her success.

"Friends are your well-wishers and they are there to keep," *mother said.*

That day, in her room, a thoughtful Priya took out an old shoe whose pair was broken. She covered it with a dark blue paint and made red and yellow flowers on it with green border. Having done this she made a sail with an ice crème stick and coloured plastic paper. She put that into the old shoe. The little waste shoe had now turned into a beautiful sail boat and on its sail little Priya wrote sincerely,

"I am SORRY."

That evening Priya went personally to Shaina who was playing in her garden with other friends and presented the sail boat to her. The blue boat sailed in a small pond in Shaina's garden and it sailed round and round with the wind. Shaina and the other friends clapped for Priya's creativity and originality.

"You are really a good painter and very creative too," Shaina said.

"Even I would like to have a sail boat like this,"Aditi requested.

"Me too," Richa shouted.

"And . . . . I just want to stay with all of you," Priya told all her friends.

Now Priya does not brag about her photograph, autograph and celebrity status to her friends and they all love and respect her for her unique capabilities.

4

A straw hat

It was a summer evening and the children had come to the ground to play. Tia joined their group just then with a beautiful red straw hat on her head.

The hat looked pretty on her. The straws were knitted into a unique design and the blue, green ribbons at the border made the hat a very different piece.

Boodhi, the goat, was also in the ground. Her kind master had let her out alone.

The goat was beside herself with happiness. She drank in the sun and the wind and ran across the ground in a high spirit. She enjoyed her blissful freedom and trotted up to a high mound covered with the green grass.

Tia wanted to play the 'Leap goat' with Boodhi. She chased the little goat and brought her down in her arms. She made Raghu sit on all fours and made the goat leap over him. But Boodhi was very young and she also did not know the game,

—Bump! Bump!!

She fell over on to her back and was very upset.

"Baa . . . . !" she cried and little Raghu and Sonu came to her rescue.

"Boodhi does not like this game." They told Tia and gave the goat some tender grass to eat.

The two boys decided to make a Goat-Cart with Boodhi. They brought the wheel cart from their garden and tied a rope loosely around her. They hitched Boodhi to the cart and off they went around the ground for their fun ride.

The other children found it very amusing—a goat pulling a cart.

"Come on run, little goat," shouted the delighted kids.

But Boodhi was very unhappy. She stood on her hind leg in protest and lo, poor children fell on the ground with a thud.

Boodhi galloped away with all her might then and the children let her go this time.

"Come on, let's play Hide and Seek," called Tia and kept her hat on the grass.

One, two and three,

It is your turn to seek! *Tia told Sonu, the youngest of all.*

And the game began.

It was great fun to hide amongst the bushes and run and run across the field to seek. The children enjoyed the game a lot. Their cheeks were pink in the hot air and the sweat was trickling down behind their ears. The evening came quickly and it was time to go back home.

"Hey, where is my straw hat?" Tia asked.

And the children started looking for it around the park. They searched up and down but nobody could find it anywhere. The hat had simply vanished.

Suddenly Raghu noticed Boodhi sitting near another ride and munching something very fast.

"Hey, what is there in Boodhi's mouth?" he shouted.

But Boodhi munched and munched and there was a gleam in her eyes.

"Boodhi!" requested Tia, "please show me at least what you are eating!"

And the goat cried,

"Ba . . . . !"

Tia's beautiful hat had really become a tasty dessert for the angry goat—the ribbons and the flowers were particularly tasty.

5

Not me

Ninni and Dia, the two sisters were off on their holidays to the country. They were invited to stay with their grandmother and they wished to see the farms, the ponds and the animals. The girls sang in excitement,

Ducks, parrots and crow,

Where wheat on the land, farmers grow!

Up to the hill and down to the pond,

We would go round and round!!

Grandmother was a fine lady. She lived in a cottage in the middle of a small village all by herself. Every morning, she went for a walk with a little basket hung on her arm and did all her shopping herself. She then cooked for the day and took care of the house.

At 7 am, the first day, when Dia and her little sister Ninny were still sleeping granny came in and asked,

"Good morning, who is going to help me to make the bed?"

Covering her eyes with both of her hands, a lazy Dia cried, "Not me!" She then turned her head and fell off to sleep.

"May I?" little Ninni got up immediately and asked politely. She picked up the other end of the bed sheet then to help.

Granny was preparing the breakfast for the kids some time later. She baked soft muffins and made cheese sandwiches and called the children lovingly,

"Who is going to lay the table for the hot breakfast?"

"Not me!" said Dia, sipping her milk leisurely. After all, it was her holidays.

And little Ninni laid the table to help granny.

After breakfast, it was time to clean the house and grandmother wanted some fresh red roses from the garden for her vase,

"Who is going to get the flowers for me?" she asked again.

"Not me!" said Dia and buried her face in the video games and little Ninni ran outside to get them.

In the afternoon, there was a movie show "Ice Age 4" in the nearby community hall. Grandmother was free. "Who is going to club to see the Ice Age?" grand mom asked the kids again.

Hurrey . . . . ! And both the girls came running to her in excitement,

"I love seeing animated movies," little Ninni told her shyly.

"So do I," the elder sister Dia said and asked eagerly, "Shall we change granny?"

"Wait! Wait, not so fast, first tell me, who made the bed?" granny asked Dia.

"Errr . . . . rrr . . . . !"

"Not me!"Dia said slowly.

"And who laid the breakfast table in the morning?"

"Hmmmm . . . Not me!"Dia said more slowly.

"And who brought the roses from the garden for me?"

"Well . . . . ! Not me! Ninni did that too," said Dia in a voice close to a whisper.

Dia's grandmother, with a winsome smile, told her, "Dia, your daily job of doing household work can't be wished away. All you need to have is a little empathy in your heart and a smile on your lips to make a cheerful day. Ninni will come with me to see the movie as she has both."

And from that day to this day, Dia has never been lazy again!

6

The first lesson

It was his first day to school and little Maan was frightened to leave the familiar surroundings of his home for an unknown world.

"Mom, I want to stay with you. I don't want to go to school," he wailed.

Mother promised Maan a new toy or some puzzle and said she would take him later on a metro ride but nothing could persuade him to go to a place called 'school'. He cried and cried and agreed only when mom promised to be there with him till he was comfortable.

And the moment they reached the play school 'Tender Heart', little Maan was most happy than ever. Contrary to what the tiny boy had imagined, the school was a wonderful place.

A huge giraffe was carrying an umbrella just near the gate. Snug in their little pots, the young pansies were blooming. There was a red and grey elephant, holding a slide in his big mouth and a green toad with a bow and tie was practicing high jump in the fountain.

"It must be such fun," he sighed, "playing at school."

One naughty boy, who was an old student of the school, came there and pushed a dreamy eyed Maan on purpose. Maan fell down. He looked at his mother but chose not to cry. He got up and pushed the naughty boy too. The boy also fell down and pushed Maan once again. But Maan did not mind this time either, he was listening carefully to a brown bear tapping away on his drum.

Mother took Maan to his class, the drum beat was the indication of that only.

He looked inside the room, it was dark and the teacher was not smiling. Maan felt like crying again, it was time to leave dear mother. Suddenly Maan noticed another boy tugging on to his mother's saree and yelling louder. He did not want to go to the class either!

Little Maan had an idea,

"Come on, let's go in together," he told the boy.

Bidding their mothers 'Good Bye' the two nervous pupil went into their classroom slowly but they did not know where to sit. The teacher told the weeping child to sit next to her and told Maan to sit next to one of the girls as there was no other seat.

The teacher gave the children the books of rhymes and asked them to recite the poem after her. Maan was idly turning over the pages when suddenly his rhyme book began to juggle with its pages. And all the letters started dancing before his eyes. The letter 'A' jumped, 'T' .... hopped and 'S' somersaulted on his table and then the letter 'o' .... yawned looking at him.

Little Maan heard the girl sitting next complaining,

"Ma'am, this boy has fallen asleep."

Every one began to laugh, even the boy sitting next to the teacher laughed.

Startled, Maan picked up his rhyme book, which had slipped down to the floor.

Maan was about to cry again but then it all seemed very funny to him and he also laughed loudly. And lo, the teacher laughed too. She said,

"Good! I was afraid that you would start crying."

"So was I," Maan whispered.

"Now children, I want you to remember that when you feel like crying, you should try to laugh."

That was the first lesson Maan learnt in the school on the first day.

7

The garden after the rain

The young lily was lying dormant inside the hard soil in Neema's garden for long. She was hungry and thirsty and was afraid of the darkness around. She could smell the scents of the spring and she moaned to push herself up. But the soil atop was not soft.

It was late April and the summer was in its full peril. The hot sun had parched the earth to the core. The flowers were wilted, the green grass was paled and the frogs were burrowed deep into the ground away from the blazing sun. They were all praying silently for the rains but it was still a month or two for the monsoon to arrive.

Though Neema watered the garden twice a day but it was not adequate, it had become a barren piece of depleted land.

Up in the sky, suddenly a patch of dark cloud appeared and Neema's friend, a brown sparrow, whispered something in the mighty eagle's ear. Lo, the big bird flew high up to the black mist and requested it to rain.

The generous cloud threw a shadow over the garden soon and a summer storm followed the next. The gutsy wind blew later with thunder and lightning. And—Big drops of water splashed down then on the thirsty garden.

Rain, what a wonderful rain! Neema exclaimed.

She came out in the garden and was drenched in no time. She looked at the kind hearted sparrow which had taken shelter in her letter box and they both smiled at each other fondly.

With the summer rain lashing at the garden, the birds sat silently and enjoyed the gust, the plants moved back and forth in gaiety and the frogs came out croaking. The colours came back to the balsam and the leaves were green at last.

When it had done all it wanted, the little cloud said goodbye to the sparrow and went on its way to drop a little of its precious rain on some other needy garden.

Neema waved the black cloud with her little white handkerchief and sang,

> **Big-big cloud, old and grey,**
>
> **It is so wonderful, that you rained,**
>
> **Now birdies dance and froggies play,**
>
> **Thank you, cloud, for a blissful day.**

When the sun came out again, there were puddles everywhere in the garden and the rainbow shone brilliantly in each of them.

A kind earthworm heard lily's sob just then and took pity. He dug all around the top soil over the bulb and made a hole. A good hearted snail put his trail to show her the way it ran from down to the top. The young lily trotted up to meet the spring and she smiled for joy. She could see a lush garden around and a beautiful rainbow above.

The flowers shook off their raindrops in brilliant flashes of colours over little lily— Just to welcome her.

8

Speedy, my wonderful horse

Speedy was a beautiful white wooden horse in Milli's play school and she loved riding on him each day.

The horse was the best thing in her class and Milli found in him a true friend with whom she was comfortable with. His black eyes were faithful and his behavior was gentle. And little Milli doted on him the most in the whole school.

Although Milli didn't know, how the real horse would behave, but Speedy was more loving and caring than even a real horse, she was sure. She rode on his bare back with no saddle, bridle and harness and the faithful Speedy listened to her command, no matter what!

With Speedy, Milli rode over all the imaginary mountains, jumped all the deep seas and played the most exciting games for hours. Clutching Speedy's mane tightly Milli sang often,

> **I have a little pony,**
>
> **Speedy is his name,**
>
> **I ride on him all the day,**
>
> **Little children-get away!**

When the other children saw little Milli enjoying so much on Speedy, they would crowd around them and say,

"Oh! What a beautiful horse Speedy is! Let us also play on it!"

"No you won't!" A possessive Milli would cry.

"It is my horse."

"Go away! Don't you touch my horse, Go! Go . . . ."

Milli would then scream so loudly that even Ma'am Reena would request the children to let the Speedy be with her only. She knew well that Milli was new to the class and would take a long time to adjust with other children.

But Speedy, the wooden horse was growing old. His paint was wearing off and his black eyes were showing signs of it being used long. His white coat was paled and the brown hooves looked tired and fatigued and . . . one day, to every one's surprise, an another teacher came and told the class,

"We are going to remove Speedy from here, it has become old."

"No!" howled Milli. And she cried so much that it was difficult to stop her then.

Mark, Milli's class mate decided to help. He and his four friends tried to work on the old, haggard horse,

"I have got some paint in the house." Bobby said.

"And, I know painting." Mustafa declared. They all gathered around Speedy the next day and got him painted in deep red colour. Milli's teacher Ms Reena gave some black colour to paint his eyes, tail and mane.

Wow!!

Milli's beautiful horse, Speedy, now looked more beautiful than before and thankfully, no one came to take him away from her.

Milli hugged Speedy with pleasure. She was thrilled. She settled down on top of Speedy to take a ride but then she shouted unexpectedly,

"Who will take the ride on Speedy first?"

"Me! Me!! Me!!!"

Ha! Ha!! . . . . All the children shouted together and crowded Speedy. The children had had great fun and Speedy carried each one of them safely.

From then on Milli always shares her things with her friendly classmates. And she is no more a possessive girl.

9

The toys world

*I*t was Christmas time. Snug and warm inside her fur coat, little Nehal came to the shopping mall with her mother and got stuck, gazing up at the beautiful toys kept in the shop's window. Nehal thought as if she was dreaming-In front of her there stood the best of the toys, all lit up with real stars.

A huge Christmas tree was placed at the center of the window and the white and blue moon was perched on its top. The beautiful dolls were busy in their kitchen.

The trains, the cars and the aero-planes were carrying gifts wrapped in beautiful papers. The busy bees with large antennas were humming and just below the green caterpillars were loitering all over the Christmas tree.

Trot . . . Tr . . . . o . . . t!

On each corner of the window, there were flowers and chocolates, and then there were colourful streamers all around. The toy world was full of magic and dream.

"Oh, I love them so much" Nehal told her mother earnestly," And I wish to have them all for my room." But mother of course, refused.

And lo, soon little Nehal flew into temper and started howling.

"Ho, Ho . . . Ho!" Ringing a bell, Santa Clause appeared from behind the toy window with a huge red sack. He wished Christmas to her joyously and gave her a fine doll. The lovely doll with blue dress was attached with a label that said,

Magic Smiles!

And in small print it explained: "This doll magically converts tears into smiles."

Wow! That was great and the moment the teary eyed Nehal looked at the doll, she smiled and casted a spell on Nehal and that made Nehal smile too.

Nehal cried, but this time for joy.

The next day, on the Christmas Eve, little Nehal set out to work. She carried her new doll and some toys in a basket and ran down the lane, outside her house. She was looking for someone who was unhappy and crying. She soon came upon a street girl who was weeping disconsolately. She was hurt.

Nehal gave her the magical doll and the injured girl was spell bound to feel happy. Both the girls spent a fun time together playing and talking, and when they parted, they parted as friends.

Something similar happened with Radha aunty who came in her house for the work. She dropped and broke some plates and felt like crying. Nehal gave her the magical doll and Radha soon stopped being upset.

Nehal's old grandfather who couldn't find his walking stick was also unhappy.

"I am so old—my arthritis is so painful!" He cried.

"Nonsense," said Nehal and gave him her doll. The spell cheered him up too and he was smiling once again.

Since then Nehal realized that cheering up people and sharing happiness with them is much more valuable than collecting toys and dolls and that is the true spirit of all the festivals.

10

Potato chips

Shibu and Sara were happy kids—they had the best Mom in the world. They liked her a lot and called her 'Super Mom' lovingly.

Super Mom was the children's best friend.

She taught them to clean out their cupboards, helped them in doing their home-works and narrated good stories to them each night. And moreover she had a solution for their all known and unknown problems.

Once Sara brought a hurt puppy home from the road, mother gave him warm milk to drink and put the dressing on him.

And when Ms William, Shibu's teacher, made him rewrite 'U' two, three times on the board and the children laughed at his bad handwriting, mom taught him how to hold his pencil correctly and to go straight up and down, crossing the "t's" and dotting the "I's", properly.

"When we love someone, we want to give him the best that we have-

It may be the biggest piece of cake or may be just a hug or could be a Surprise Birthday party!"

And a surprise party was arranged for mom on her Birthday and she had promised to not to enter the kitchen until everything was ready. Sara and Dad were cooking something special for the dinner and Shibu sang joyously,

Today is not the same as it was before,

And we are busy all the more,

We are so happy for this day,

It's Super Mom's Happy Birthday.

Sara peeled off lots of big potatoes to fry them into hot chips and Dad mixed the cake batter and put that in an oven. And little Shibu told his father,

"I would sprinkle salt over the fried chips and then it will be fine to call mother inside."

The table was set, the cake was decorated, and a candle was lit to sparkle on the table with all its light and beauty. A restless Shibu climbed the chair to reach the cupboard and took out a blue salt cellar from the shelf.

"Steady!" Dad and Sara cried together loudly.

Errr . . . . ,

It was too late a call.

Little Shibu had sprinkled sugar all over the crispy potato chips by mistake.

And lo and Behold,

Mother came inside just then.

"Did you all say ready?" she asked. And everyone laughed at that and told her what had happened.

"Well, that is how good dishes are invented," mom said smiling.

And with the birthday cake, Shibu's sugar-chips were delicious for they had in them the invaluable love of the family.

11

Forgetful Rhea

*R*hea was a forgetful girl. She would never listen carefully and often forgot what was told to her.

Once Rhea bought a birthday present for his grandfather and forgot to whom to present. And once Rhea was playing 'Hide and Seek' and she climbed on a tree, covered herself nicely with leaves and then she slept. She forgot completely that she was playing and her friends were looking for her.

One day, science teacher, Ms Das Gupta gave little Rhea some bean seeds to grow in her kitchen garden.

"These bean seeds will show you the different stages of germination and you will get some green vegetables to eat too," madam told Rhea lovingly.

She also told her as how to plant the seeds in detail and how to take care of the saplings later.

Little Rhea was excited. She soon found a small plot of earth in her kitchen garden for her seeds. She watered the area, put little manure, put the seeds and covered them with the soil.

Aw . . . . !

Poor Rhea but forgot what the seeds were and what their name was.

Her grand pa saw her working in the garden first. She was working devotedly with her tiny spade. He came close to inspect.

"Oh! Are you growing turnips?" he asked.

"Errr . . . ! Yes!" Rhea said with a little doubt.

Her mother visited her plot the next. And when she saw some green shoots coming out of the earth, she thought them to be radish.

"These radishes are going to be good," mother said affectionately.

"Oh thank you, mom," said Rhea unsure.

Father said the plants were tomatoes and grand mum chuckled that they were peas. A confused Rhea did nothing but agreed with all of them.

After a long-long wait, when the beans finally came out, the whole family shouted together in one voice,

. . . . BEANS!

"Hey, they are beans!" they all cried and laughed.

"Errr . . . . Yeah," Rhea said shyly.

"That is what my science teacher told."

And Rhea never forgot this incident ever. She eventually improved and remembered to listen carefully.

12

Peeping monster

*E*veryone in her neighbourhood called her 'a shy baby'; young Aaruni was not just shy, she was very very shy.

When guests came to her house and asked her name, she would dig her chin into her neck and not speak else she would hide behind her mother and close her eyes or she would just run out of that room.

In school too she preferred to sit at the far end of the class so that Ms Daisy, her class teacher, might not spot her. And when Ms Daisy did notice her and asked her about something, she would pretend as if she were not listening.

One day, in her recitation class, Ma'am asked her to recite a poem. Little Aaruni was panic stricken. First she did not get up from her place and when Misha, the girl sitting next to her pushed her, she dragged her leaden feet and reached where ma'am was sitting, to recite the poem.

Twinkle . . . . Twinkle . . . Twi . . . Twi . . .

Little Aaruni turned as white as a sheet out of fear. The class started spinning, her mouth went dry and then there was a strange buzz in her ears of her heart beat.

Ma'am told her gently to practice the poem more at home.

"Why did you not recite the poem, you have learnt so well, in the class?" her mother asked in the evening.

"Mom, when the teacher asked me to recite in front of all the smart children, a monster came out from the teacher's back and snarled at me. He made me forget all my lines," Aaruni told her mother shyly.

"And how does this monster look like?" mother asked her curiously.

"Err . . . Sometimes it is like you and sometimes it is like Ms Daisy," Aaruni told her little more shyly now.

Aaruni's mother could understand a bit as how her shy baby must be feeling in the school. She suggested,

"Look Aaruni, I'll tell you a secret, if you look straight out of the class and look at the clouds, birds, trees and flowers, you would not be afraid of the monsters and you can then recite the poem that you know so well like other smart girls in your class."

Aaruni accepted.

She knew she would need to be brave to think about other things and then speak but she wanted to give a try. She herself wanted to be bold.

During the next recitation evaluation, when Ma'am told Aaruni to recite the poem, Aaruni looked outside the window in the class, and lo . . . . , she could not find a bird or a cloud or a flower. She closed her eyes then and whispered,

> **"I wish, if I could,**
>
> **If I could, I would.**
>
> **I would not because I could not . . . ."**

"Oh, we have a real poet in our class," said Daisy Ma'am warmly and Aaruni opened her eyes to see the admiring looks in her class friends' faces and then she dared further,

> **"I would not because I could not.**
>
> **Because I am very shy,**
>
> **I am like a birdie,**
>
> **I whisper in reply."**

The teacher and the children clapped and clapped for her beautiful original poem.

At home little Aaruni was happy. When an anxious mom asked her about the peeping and teasing monster during the test, little Aaruni replied a little less shyly now,

"Yeah mom, the monster was there at the teacher's back, but he told me to speak my own lines."

13

Speak and listen

*A*bid did not know how to talk properly—he just used to shout. He was angry with every one put together and each person separately.

When someone would say, "Why are you pecking at your food?" he would feel hurt and when someone would say, "Why are you stuffing yourself with food like that?" he would then also feel offended and get into temper and when he got into temper, which was often, he would yell and kick at anything near him. And his parents did not know how to control his temper. And another thing that Abid did not like was using the word 'Sorry' and 'Excuse me.'

"Why I must say sorry at all?" he wondered aloud.

One day, his uncle Peter had an idea; he bought a talking parrot, Pickoe and taught him phrases like,

"Abid is always angry."

"Abid never says sorry."

"Abid makes noise when he is shouting." And so on. He presented Pickoe to Abid and never told a word about what the parrot had been taught. Abid, the little boy, was thrilled with the gift.

Abid was taken to the circus the next day by his school. It was very interesting and little Abid liked there 'Talking Parrot' the best. He decided there to tame his pet then and teach him some words to speak too, "It would be fun if my Pickoe could also speak and listen."

And the next Sunday, Abid came out with Pickoe in his sunny garden with lots of chilies. The pet loved the green chilies a lot. Abid told his pet,

"Come along my little pet,

Chilies are fun, so I bet!

Follow my lips and learn some word,

Without them, you are but a nerd."

The parrot was glad to be out in the lush garden. And when he was offered chilies, for speaking small words like 'Hello', 'Come here' he repeated them quickly and tweaked with laughter. Abid was happy, he was a good trainer, he thought.

He took his training seriously and tried to teach Pickoe—a shake hand. He held the pet's one foot up with his one hand and took chili in another hand. He would not give chili to the pet unless he said, 'Hello!' with one foot up. Pickoe was one foot up for long and chili was far from his reach;

Pickoe was uncomfortable and he refused to listen. Abid became angry, he shouted, "You are banished from the garden. And from now on you will not be given any chilies too."

Ahem . . . . ! Pickoe was tired and he became angry too. He jumped up and bit Abid in his finger.

"Ow! He bit me!" Abid screamed loudly.

"Ow!! He was shouting at me!" the parrot screamed louder than him.

Abid was frightened. He had never heard a parrot speaking so clearly except in circus and so frightened was he that he ran inside his house and left his 'Talking Parrot' in the garden only. Night came and a cold parrot shivered in the open, he did not understand why Abid was torturing him like this. Now it was his turn to complain to everyone put together and each person separately around,

"Abid hates being polite."

"Abid never says sorry."

"Abid makes noise when he is shouting."

Pickoe made so much of noise that the whole neighborhood got collected to see as to why was Abid troubling his poor pet so much? The parrot was pacified only when little Abid said sorry that too in front of everyone.

When Uncle Peter called again, mother told him, "Abid is not an angry boy any more. He says 'sorry' and 'excuse me' always and doesn't get offended soon." He speaks so softly and politely that Pickoe has learnt to say,

"Abid can you speak a little louder, I can't hear you."

14

Food combo

Aahan had two special hobbies—*eating good food and going to a good restaurant.*

He was always looking up for something fried and he liked burgers, potato rolls, pastas and pitzas. But sadly . . . . he did not like his daily food-rice, chapatti and curry.

Aahan never ate his bread at dinner or at lunch. He would always roll his chapatti into tiny balls and throw them to the birds or else he would hide the bread under the table cover when no one noticed. He had decided that when he grew up, he would never eat chapatti and rice.

Aahan's mother was a good cook and she always made whatever Aahan asked for. And Aahan's dad often took them out for dinner in hotels.

One night, Aahan's family had their dinner in a '5 Star Hotel'. It was very tasty.

Aahan was so happy that before going to bed that night, he knelt down on the floor and prayed, "God, I wish that you make my father in-charge of the kitchen of a hotel so that I would get such tasty food daily."

Lo, and behold,

God heard his prayers, more or less, and dad took over the charge of the big kitchen in their house only.

"Mother is down with viral, get ready fast on your own and come to the kitchen," Dad commanded early morning.

Aahan was happy. He was expecting a great meal that day. But dad served little Aahan milk, toast and a boiled egg for the breakfast.

"Dad I don't like toast and milk, and I want some pasta or cheese rolls," Aahan requested.

"No!" dad told him firmly, "they are very heavy for breakfast."

In the afternoon, Aahan was served again the dry chapatti, dal, curry and rice by his dad. "Dad, I don't like this food," he pleaded, "mom always served me pasta with cheese sandwiches and potato rolls." But dad would not listen.

"Eat your lunch immediately, or I won't give you anything else," he said strictly.

And then . . . . a terrible thing happened there in the kitchen. A loving Aahan and an ever patient dad were at their worst.

"I don't want to eat this food," Aahan shouted.

"Yes you do," said Dad.

"No, I don't ," little Aahan said and threw his plate of rice and chapati on the floor.

A . . . . hem!

Dad was very angry. And he was so angry that he did not speak a word. He kept looking at him in silence. It was worse than if he had scolded.

"You have learnt to read and write but you have not learnt to respect the food! People work hard to grow grains and make bread, and you throw them on the floor-shame on you," he said finally and left.

Next many a days, till mom was unwell, Aahan was served pasta, burger and pitza day and night and he felt thoroughly ashamed of himself. Moreover, when he had lunch and dinner without rice, chapatti, egg or milk he never felt all that healthy.

Little Aahan turned to God again for help. "God, mother is a better cook, please make her fine."

And mom was back in the kitchen the very next day. She served Aahan the cheese roll in the breakfast with toast, egg and milk. Little Aahan ate all the food kept in his plate without complain. He was happy and satisfied. He also apologized to dad and made peace.

Aahan respects his food now and never throws it or hides it under the mat. He calls rice and chapatti with pasta a Mom and Dad combo and understands that farmers work hard to grow grains.

15

Cricket T-5

*P*ari and Padam never got along well with each other. Padam as a rule tried to keep away from all the girls in his class and Pari noticed it and began to tease him for it. And that is how it all started.

Pari often played practical jokes on him and they were not always in the best of taste. Once, Pari told Padam that he had won the first prize in drawing competition, Padam went all the way to the office to collect it but there weren't anyone there—and no prizes either.

During intervals too, little Pari would not leave him alone. She would sit at his desk with her friends and howled with laughter. Padam would become red in his face. The other boys would suggest,

"Why do you pay attention to her just yell her off!"

But little Padam never yelled at her. He would avoid her more and more and would cry hiding his face with his hands.

But that day, all his patience was gone into drain. Padam hit her hard with his rubber ball and the ball got accurately planted where it was aimed—on Pari's forehead. It was now little Pari's turn to hide her face and cry in anguish.

Some boy called out in the play ground,

"I suppose, Padam aimed well, Pari nearly lost her smile!"

Everyone laughed. But Padam was given punishment and told to write 'No Violence' a hundred times by his class-teacher Ms Jyoti.

The matter was serious. And it so happened that a 'Junior Cricket T-5' was being played in between the two sections of class two in the play ground. Pari, like always, started teasing Padam for being the slowest runner in his team. She was laughing and giggling with her friends and all her silly comments were directed at him and for him only.

Taking her pranks with coolness, Padam played on with all his concentration. But when he was chasing a ball to stop an extra run for his team, she commented loudly, "Look, Padam would surely miss the aim. He can't throw a ball straight."

And all her friends joined her and started calling out,

> **"Padam can't throw a ball straight.**

> **So she says, so she says**

> **For hours and hours he tries and plays,**

> **So she says, so she says.**

> **Padam can't throw a ball straight."**

Little Padam was most unhappy. "I can," he thought.

"Show us a good throw," cried Pari again.

"All right, then see." he mumbled. And in an instant, he threw his ball straight at Pari, just to prove a point.

Lo, and Behold.

Everything fell silent. Seeing Pari's swollen forehead, the game was stopped and an angry ma'am gave punishment to Padam.

Back in the class one of Pari's friends got up and told ma'am everything truthfully.

"Is there anything you can do other than hitting, if someone is always troubling you?" Jyoti ma'am asked.

"No!" little Padam spoke honestly.

"You can be either firm or complain, but if you hit, you are no better than her," said she, *"and remember children, two wrongs don't make a right."*

Jyoti Ma'am told Pari to write the same thing, hundred times. She had shown mental violence to Padam too.

16

A drawing test

Joe was an unhappy child that day—there was a drawing test in his school the next day and he did not want to be there. The children always made fun of his drawings, no matter what!

Little Joe knew well that whatever he made in his test—the hut, the tree, the kite or the flower, he would be laughed at. His drawing was really bad and he cried in despair, "I don't want to learn, read and write I am happy in my home."

When Joe was small he always dreamt of going to school and loved spending all his time in drawing. He loved making houses, huts, trees and birds.

But his trees, birds and the huts were always hideous, crooked and hunch backed. Not a single line he drew was straight up and down. Unfortunately, when little boy was given a box of crayons to colour, his colour scheme was equally poor and his all houses would be blue, chimneys-yellow, trees-red and the birds green and . . . The smoke that came out of the chimney of his houses would always be pink.

These drawings were pretty pictures for him. But anyone who came to his house, would always ask,

"Joe, where did you ever see the red trees and the green birds?"

"In this picture," Joe would reply innocently. No one appreciated his drawings in his home but no one chided too. And his loving mother encouraged him to make more and more houses with more and more trees.

But in the school things were different. Joe drew so poorly that when the boys saw his drawings, a ripple of laughter would run right through them. Ms Leena, his drawing teacher's face would become all puckered in a frown as if she had eaten a sour lemon. And little Joe would feel very hurt and sore himself.

Some of the kind girls felt sorry for him and when the teacher turned her back they would quickly draw something in his drawing book. They tried to do their worst but no one could draw as badly as Joe. The teacher would notice the difference immediately and Joe was honest enough to accept that it was not his work. The teacher would then say,

"Joe, you have to do it yourself."

It was a serious matter and dad had to help. He called Joe and said,

"It is all right Joe, you will be the only child in the class drawing with a bangle."

Dad took one bangle and drew a circle with its help, then he took another round 'cap' and with that he made another smaller circle on top of the first one. He made a letter 'M' on top of small circle and a zig—zag tail on a big circle and when he drew two small eyes and few straight lines as mustache in the small circle,

lo and behold-There was a cute little cat in Joe's book, staring lovingly at him.

"Wow! This is easy dad, I think I can make it. But what colour shall I use to fill it?" Joe shouted in happiness.

"Use the colours that you have seen in a real cat," dad advised him gently.

The next day, every one including Ms Leena, clapped for the beautiful kitten in black and grey colours that Joe had made in his drawing test.

It was not the best but good enough to not to be laughed about.

17

Round the world

In a small town in South Andhra, there lived Sunny and Tara the naughty twins who were always looking up for some adventure. The children made twice as much trouble as the others.

One summer evening when the sun was still hot, the twins took out their newly purchased drums and sticks and strode down the road through the colony, beating hard on them.

Rat-a Tat—Tat!

Rat a Tat—Tat!!

They beat the drums loudly with a count of four.

"Where is this band party going?" Trisha, their aunt asked.

"We are going on a trip round the world," Sunny and Tara told her with all their enthusiasm.

"Oh, is it?" she "aren't you scared, going off so far from home?"

"No!" replied the kids proudly.

"But Tommy, our big dog is loose-keep out of his way!" she warned.

"We aren't afraid of anything," the kids declared.

And all of sudden the huge Tommy appeared from a corner of the lane. He hated loud sounds and did not like—a Rat a tat—tat. He rushed towards them barking loudly.

Bow . . . . wow!

"Oh mom, help!" Tara cried.

"Let's run!" Sunny suggested.

And the little twins dropped their both of the sticks and ran as fast as they could with their bands on their head.

What a lucky escape!

Back in their house, in their garden, Sunny saw a slug slipping into the moist earth and he got another bright idea of taking 'A trip round the world'. He picked up a small spade from the back yard and started digging a small plot in his garden.

"Our earth, where we live, is round," he told Tara, "and if we keep digging from one side, we may reach America or someplace, on the other side soon."

"Oho, that's great, let's discover America then and meet aunt Shaila," cried a happy Tara. She brought a shovel from inside and started helping Sunny in his discovery of America.

The children were happy. They were having great fun with digging. They worked hard and dug up a large area but suddenly little Tara jumped to her feet and yelled loudly,

"There is a snake—a big snake! Oh mom, please help."

Sunny jumped to his feet too. There was a brown snake, a feet long, crawling near Tara's feet. This was the first time he had seen a snake in his life.

Little Tara kept screaming louder and louder and the snake was crawling nearer and nearer. Sunny was frightened too but he had to protect his sister. And lo, Sunny hit it hard with his sharp spade and chopped it into two.

But—then each half of the reptile started crawling off by itself.

It was a terrible scene.

"Oh, mom, please come." Tara wailed.

Sunny was now hard at work, so first he made four snakes then he made eight from four, but neither the snake nor Tara was quiet.

"Stop it!" Mother came and held Sunny's hand firmly. "It's a grass snake. It's not poisonous," she said. Sunny stopped but little Tara continued screaming even then,

"It is grass snake! Oh Mom, please help!"

Mother pulled the kids inside the home, they had had enough adventures for one day. Their trip round the world was crashed at least for that day.

18

Motivation

*T*aanu had, off late, become a big concern for his parents. He was a couch potato and binged on ice cream, pizza, burgers, and candy. His diet lacked all the essential nutrients and his weight was around 65 kilograms.

One morning, refusing his breakfast as usual, Taanu was hungry at ten o'clock. His mother had gone out for shopping and the little boy searched his big kitchen up and down for something good to eat and . . . what luck!

Taanu found a huge packet of fried peanuts there in a box that he liked a lot.

He gulped it down fast. But the spicy nuts did no good to an empty stomach. At lunch Taanu was feeling heavy and by the evening he was down with indigestion. A worried mother sent for the doctor soon.

"The best remedy for him is not pills or injections, but a daily routine of some healthy exercise." Doctor Uncle suggested and advised him to eat light food for few days. And little Taanu agreed reluctantly to go to the playground for jogging as soon as he recovered.

But running for Taanu was as boring as torturous. The first day itself, he found it difficult to run and jog without a reason. There should be some motivation to run, he thought. And suddenly, he noticed his class mate Anuj, at corner of the park, jogging like a rabbit. He would come daily to the ground for fresh air.

"Err . . . . Anuj, can you teach me some simple exercises? It is difficult for me to run on my own," Taanu went close to him and requested.

And Anuj, a good friend, took up his job rather seriously.

"Bend over and touch your toes a few times!" said Anuj without wasting a moment. He himself bent up and down a few times to draw Taanu's attention to these easy and interesting exercises.

But Taanu with a big paunch found them more difficult than running.

The next day Anuj came up with a different plan and suggested,

"Try these, they are basic." He kicked his left leg up then to touch his right hand.

Ah . . . . ! But for Taanu they were difficult again. He struggled hard with his left leg and toppled over. He was hurt and did not want to continue.

The third day a clever Anuj brought a packet of fried peanuts and told Taanu seriously, "I will give you this packet if you are able to catch me."

And Anuj started running without waiting for his response.

Well—this was a good enough reason for Taanu to run. And an ever hungry Taanu, started chasing Anuj for the fried peanuts in the morning.

After 10 minutes of this chase for the packet, Taanu sped up and caught Anuj and demanded his well-earned peanuts.

"Hey! I gave you the motivation to run; if you want this packet, you have to run one more round." Anuj said encouragingly. And little Tanu then completed one more lap of his real . . . motivated . . . exercise—for a small packet of peanuts.

Within 5 days Taanu and his motivator Anuj picked up the rhythm and up went their running graph. Taanu slowly found a new joy in coming to the ground daily and he also felt better from within.

19

The annual day

Saify's house off late had became very noisy and one could hear little girl's baritone from the front gate itself,

"Who knows who knows?

Where the sun goes,

And what does he do all day?"

Saify was selected as one of the singers for a group song on her 'Annual Day' and she was very nervous about it. She had never been on a stage before but she had promised herself to do well.

Little Saify believed in hard work and so she practiced day and night. She practiced the song in her play time, practiced it in her meal time, sleep time and . . . . dream time and no one knows just how many times.

When Saify practiced the first day, the kitchen door of her house squeaked mystically with her song. The clock in the dining room clicked the beat. And the wooden staircase creaked a magical note.

"Creak! Click!! Squeak !"

"Creak! Click!! Squeak!!!" spoke them all.

Finding these sounds, a perfect match to her practice, Saify let the kitchen door open ajar so that it may squeak louder. She walked up and down on the stairs for the woods to creak and she set the alarm to let the clock ring with her song always.

And thus, she created her own orchestra to practice with.

On the 'Annual Day' the group song, of standard one, was the last item of the evening. The parents, the friends and the audience started clapping and cheering up the group as the little singers appeared on the stage one by one,. The dresses of the kids were bright and complimenting their item perfectly.

Little Saify came and sat in the center, holding everyone's attention. She was looking beautiful in her pink gown and a green cap.

And just as the tiny tots were about to start—Tina a young girl of the group, tripped over a wire.

Lo and behold,

The well lit auditorium plunged into darkness. The music stopped, the orchestra band stopped and a hush fell upon the huge hall. The little singers waited nervously on the stage. They had no idea as to how to go about singing without the mike and the band.

But Saify was not afraid. She took a deep breath, cleared her throat and began loud and clear.

> **"Who knows who knows?**
>
> **Where the sun goes,**
>
> **And what does he do all days?**
>
> **He talks to the flowers, for hours and hours,**
>
> **And gives the leaves, green colour away!!"**

Other children followed the lead quickly and the audience smiled wide-eyed.

They gave the children their best beat with claps and thumps. They also tossed flowers on the stage and joined them in that last song of the evening.

Saify won praises with her perfect performance. And her hard work paid her rich dividends indeed.

64

20

A beautiful garland

Aapti and Anshi leapt from their bed, dashed to the kitchen to have breakfast and ran to play in their garden. It was a warm sunny day and the school was closed for three days long.

"What shall we play on such a wonderful day?" Aapti asked.

"Let us see, how many kinds of flowers we can find in our garden," Anshi replied.

It was early winter and the garden was in full bloom. The two girls looked carefully around and picked just a few flowers of each variety, so that there would be plenty left in the beds to grow. Still they had flowers of many colours there—the red Poppies, white and purple Flocks, pink Daffodils, orange Nasturtium and violet Pansies. The girls collected them all and strung them together to make a garland for their mother.

"Oh, what is there?" Aapti shouted with pleasure. Some healthy mushrooms had grown under the rose bushes. The girls plucked them too and put them neatly in their baskets with the garland.

"Please help me and give me some money," a beggar clanked his begging bowl, just then, from the gate.

"Oh, our mother gives no money to the beggar," replied Anshi sadly.

"Can you give me something to eat then?" he asked.

"Of course, you can take these mushrooms. They would make lovely soup," offered Aapti and ran to give.

"Errrr . . . . , No, I don't want mushrooms," said the beggar and ran away faster.

There was a garden trolley in one corner of the garden and Aapti asked Anshi to sit in it. It was a simple two wheeled cart to take pots and manure from one place to another and now Aapti ferried Anshi from one end of the garden to other in it.

Ha! Ha . . . .

"Oh! It is so much of fun!"Anshi said enjoying the ride.

It was noon and now the girls were hungry and tired. So they came inside the house with their baskets. Mother had made special 'Vada Pav' for her little ones.

Trnnnn . . . . !

The door-bell rang just then. Pia, their neighbor was at the door. She had a small bag in her hand with some fresh and juicy carrots for them that her mother had grown in her kitchen garden.

"Pia, why can't your mother grow 'Vada Pav' in the garden? I don't like carrots," asked Anshi.

"Vada Pav?" "In the garden?" Pia was confused.

"She means you can have 'Vada Pav' with us," mom explained. The lunch was delicious and all the three children enjoyed it a lot.

"Mom, can we make some mushroom soup for Pia's mother?" remembering the mushrooms and the garland Anshi asked. She gave them to her mother.

Mother was delighted with the garland and she put it nicely around her bun. But the mushrooms were wild and poisonous and they were thrown away immediately.

"The mushrooms that we eat are grown in farms not in the wild," mom said softly.

"Oh, that is why the poor beggar did not take them," Aapti thought sadly,

"I should have given him some 'vada pav' from inside."

"I want to make a garland for my mother too," Pia said suddenly looking at the beautiful garland on her aunt.

"Sure," said Apti, "let us go and pick up some more flowers."

And lo, the girls ran to the garden again to help Pia.

"Holidays are fun," Anshi spoke happily.

"And we must have many more such days," Aapti and Pia shouted joyously together.

21

English homework

It was Tina's seventh Birthday and her mother called each one of her class mates in her house for a party.

Three of Tina's friends Sara, Vinnie and Jessy decided to give her a special present. As soon as they got back from the school, they got together in Jessy's house with her mom and set to work-mixing and stirring. By the lunch the three friends had baked a yummy chocolate cake for their best friend.

Tina, the birthday girl, was always at the top of the class in Geography. She was the best at composition too. And it was all because of her big brother Joey. Every month Joey went on a trip to a foreign country, a long way from home, and on his return, he always described every exciting detail of his adventure to her little sister, Tina.

That's how Tina always wanted to find out all about the world and when she was asked to write a composition she found it easy too. She wrote stories about his brother's exciting adventures and narrated them well. Tina was then given the name 'The Narrator' by her English teacher, Ms Jane.

"She narrates any incident so well that it becomes a story," madam would tell the class proudly.

Sara, Vinnie and Jessy lived in the same building as Tina. The school was near-by and all four walked to the school together. They shared the same bench in the class and the same hobbies at the play ground. And all the four friends helped each other if stuck with a problem.

When it was time to go to the party, the three friends wrapped and carried their cake carefully around to her house but lo . . . . , in their excitement, they forgot to do *their English homework. They were supposed to write a composition given by Ms Jane on "How I spent my Sunday."*

The girls were frightened but they thought, why worry and spoil the fun?

Tina loved their special gift a lot.

And the children had a great time throughout the lovely evening. By the time the party ended, it was night and the three friends were exhausted with playing, dancing and singing too much. But now they had something to worry too . . . . their homework.

> **Sara Vinnie and Jessy,**
>
> **Could make a cake in a jiffy!**
>
> **They would sit and think and think**
>
> **Homework would be done in a flick!!** *And so they thought.*

But that was not to happen.

"I am too tired I don't know what to write," Vinnie lamented.

"And I am feeling very sleepy," said Jessy.

They then requested Tina-the best, to help them to complete their work.

"Please Tina—we are your friends," claimed Sarah

Tina encouraged them and gave them her different ideas but all in vain. The three girls were so much burned out that little Tina had to give them her homework to copy. She was tired herself.

The next day, David mam collected their homework and when she had finished reading them she said seriously, "Here are your compositions children and they are all good but the four children—Tina, Vinnie, Sarah and Jessy wrote the best of the lot. Their compositions are very interesting and there is no mistake. In fact there is a touch of magic in them as they all have wonderful gardens, loving granny and fine pets to play with, on their Sundays."

She looked at Tina deep and hard and Tina knew that David ma'am knows all.

"The next time you four will do still better, is it clear?" the teacher warned.

Others could not understand a thing, but the four friends sitting side by side were shamed. Without being told they understood,

"If you don't do things yourself, it is dishonesty."

22

Helping hands

Saanjh and Aana decided to bake a cake for their mother one afternoon. The two girls loved exploring in the kitchen but baking could not be done by them as firstly they were young and then, they had no skills.

The girls wanted to take Mala aunty's assistance who was their house helper.

Mala aunty, however, was busy sweeping the kitchen.

The huge kitchen was in a big mess. The sink was full of soapy water and utensils and the floor was full of used napkins and vegetable peels. Mala promised to help the girls once she was done with her cleaning.

The house-maid was doing her work with all her enthusiasm. And the children did not like that. While sweeping, she was going from one corner of the kitchen to another, humming a song with a broom,

> **"Come along my sweetest broom,**
>
> **Sweeping and cleaning every room!**
>
> **Follow me and you will find,**
>
> **Lots of dust, and leave none behind!!"**

And the siblings started making fun of her excitement and energy,

"How could you do cleaning work so joyfully?" they said, "baking is much better work than cleaning." But Mala smiled and continued with her work and she did not hurry also at her task. The girls requested Mala again to leave her job but she refused.

Saanjh and Aana were angry now, they looked at each other and decided to cause nuisance to Mala for not listening to them,

"Let us give her more jobs, it will serve her right!"

They planned and started throwing papers, plastic wrappers and covers purposely on the floor to irritate her. And Rikki their pet kitten joined them too. She scattered her bread crumbs all over the kitchen to mishmash.

Mala ignored the tumult caused by them.She stopped her work suddenly, smiled mysteriously and went into another room and vanished.

"It looks, as if Mala aunty wants to play Hide and Seek with us." Saanjh wondered aloud. They ran after her but she was nowhere to be found. They looked under each bed, peeped inside each cupboard and climbed over the terrace to play hide and seek with her then.

Aha . . . . ! They all played for a long time and the children began to feel much less dismal and angry. In fact they felt very glad with Mala's company.

Mrs. Kaur came home much before her usual time and she was amazed to see her neat and clean home and busy inmates. Saanjh was washing the dishes, Aana, with a broom in her hand, was sweeping, Mala was baking and Rikki, the naughty pet was licking the bread crumbs from the floor.

And . . . . they were all humming happily,

> **"Come along my sweetest broom,**
>
> **Sweeping and cleaning every room."**

"This will make you feel less tired," said Mala serving a hot cup of tea with freshly baked cake to her mistress—Oho—the cake was delicious.

The children shared Mala's time and work and realized that if they do the work joyously, they can do it the fastest and the best.

23

A pair of parrots

Standing tall and beautiful, in a garden in twin city Hyderabad, there was a huge Gulmohar tree. He stood on the bank of a lake and was nourished well with its sweet water, naturally he was strong and massive.

During the spring each year, the Gulmohar bloomed full with flowers—red and orange, the birds loved to build their homes on him and the squirrels found holes in his trunk to store their nuts. The bees and butterflies collected nectar from his bright florets morning and evening and the mighty tree was full of life.

Just near the Gulmohar tree, there stood some wild grass too. They grew half in water and half above and had very thin stems. They flourished well in the same surroundings too but sadly they never bore any flowers big or small.

The birds and squirrels evaded treading on them for the same.

One day there was a massive storm and the strong wind broke the lively Gulmohar right from the middle. His green stem was thrown away across the water among the wild grass and in no time the blossomy tree became pale and shaky with his leaves scarcely opened.

Birds, squirrels, bees and butterflies stopped visiting him then and it appeared as if the Gulmohar was about to die.

The tree was grief stricken. To rub salt into the wounds, a wood cutter came soon with a saw and an axe and decided to sell the wood of the dead tree at good price later.

Ah . . . . !

Gulmohar's last hope of recovery was also gone.

But the tree was surprised to see the delicate grass nearby that suffered no harm at all. They not only survived the storm but also swayed in gaiety. The dying tree lamented,

"You are so frail and feeble still managed to face the wind, I was strong and took care of so many lives but got ruined."

The grass replied kindly,

"This is called destiny. You fought and failed and we bowed and were spared."

"Oh," said the mighty tree, and bowed down himself to his fate.

One fine evening, just a few days later, a pair of pretty parrots came there flying from far. They were tired. They sat down on the fallen tree to take rest. They ate the seeds kept in its hole and drank some water from the lake and perched for the night.

And . . . the next morning itself, the parrots decided to build their 'home sweet home' on the tree and brought twigs and hay for their nest.

Finding new friends, the tree was filled with a new hope.

No wonder!

Fresh sap began flowing inside and his vigour returned soon. With the first shower of the rainy season, a green shoot came out from its trunk and Gulmohar shook with happiness.

Destiny gave the tree another chance and he welcomed it with gratitude.

24

Tiger hunt

The wobbly fence between Sabal's and Sagar's house was in a bad shape. The two friends used it as a swing and rattled it about often. And more often they would play hide and seek, police thief, catch-catch around it, cracking the fence at a pole or two.

"I have had enough of climbing all over me and damaging my planks," moaned the old fence in despair.

And all the animals—brown squirrels, field mice, earthworms, frogs, snails and lots more came along to sympathize. Ginger the kitten pawed at it gently. The fence was their home sweet home and it protected them from harsh winters, blazing summers and damp monsoons.

The earthworm had an idea. He groped his way through the soil and covered the poles at one or two places with it. The treatment was slow but it helped the fence and its old joints.

One Sunday, the kids Sabal and Sagar were reading an adventure book near the fence. Suddenly they decided to play a new game 'hunt—the—tiger'. They looked at the jungle in the book long and hard. The fence in their yard almost looked like it and it was full of animals too—the squirrels, the sparrows, the rats, the snails and butterflies and lo . . . . there was a tiger too.

"Hey, see its stripes!" Sagar said with much enthusiasm looking at Ginger, the 'sleeping' kitten.

And soon their game was on.

Sagar came out in his hunter's outfit and little Sabal wore his elephant's mask. The elephant Sabal on all his fours trotted over the soft green moss and chased each and every animal put together in the jungle and little Sagar above the elephant, shot his toy gun at each animal carefully.

It was an interesting game. And the two friends took two rounds of the yard all in action. They were now looking for the Tiger.

Ginger, the kitten was resting under the fence. She had seen the kids before but not like this—the gun especially was scary.

She gazed up in wonder and so frightened was she, that she did not even try to run away. As the elephant moved towards her, Sagar fired.

Bang! Bang!

Ginger trembled and sprinted off to save her life.

And to stop the tiger slipping away, the hunter threw his gun hard on her.

Lo and behold!

The toy gun was aimed well and it hit the kitten hard, right on her little head.

She meowed loudly and—fell over. Her legs jerked and became quite. She became still then—very very still.

"Hey, we have killed the tiger," Sagar shouted. But Sabal was shocked—"No, the little kitten is dead."

All of a sudden, the children realized that the kitten had been alive and now she was dead. She would never run or jump or play with anyone any more. She would never grow up to be a big cat and she would never catch mice. She would never meow on their roof top ever. And it was all over for her just because of them.

Sagar was very angry with his friend, "it was all your idea to make the kitten a tiger," he shouted.

"And you threw . . . . your gun on him," shouted Sabal loudly.

And then . . . . both the irritated friends were fighting, shouting, kicking, chasing and charging at each other in resentment until suddenly they could not stop and . . . .

-Whoosh . . . . !

Over the kids went, face into the old fence and the fence was hit at one of its unstable pole.

Bang! Bang !

The fence too fell into pieces over the dead kitty.

Their cries brought their mothers running,

"Be quiet, both of you!" and, "What are you fighting for?"And, oh, at last they saw the kitten, lying on the earth with its eyes closed.

Sabal's mom picked up the kitten and wrapped her arms around her lovingly. For still more warmth, she put her long woolen scarf round her as well.

Oho . . . ! The clever kitty opened her eyes . . . , jumped down . . . . and dashed off . . . .

Sagar's mother shifted the old fence to her back garden. It gets climbed upon still, but not by the naughty children. Her red roses climb round its wooden posts and make it feel very happy.

And from then on, the children, Sagar and Sabal have never hurt a cat or a dog or any other plant in their life.

25

Pitter patter in the rain

*I*t was a cloudy evening and the monsoon showers were doing pitter patter on the roof. There was no power supply in the colony and the children had run out of games to play in-door. They were all huddled in a group by the candle.

"What shall we do now?" Aahna asked.

Little Daksh had an idea, they would all play the shadow game and tell each other about their future plan.

Daksh went near the lit candle first and the shadows he made with his fingers became the characters in his story. "When I grow up," he said, "I want to become a brave watch man taking care of my colony at night."

The others sat on the floor and watched his inspiring story with action.

Aahna wrapped around her mother's saree, put on her high heeled sandals and came forward for her act. Ha ha ha . . . . ! The children enjoyed her get-up too but before she could even start her show, Tim shouted,

"I don't like this story unless you bring real snacks, I am hungry."

And little Aahna ran inside and brought a tray of juice and cakes. The children devoured the cakes and enjoyed their snack party a lot. Ninni got up suddenly alarmed. Her pet dog was missing from the room. The party was stopped and the children ran outside immediately to look for him.

"Spotty, Spotty, where are you?" shouted the children.

"woof!" whimpered Spotty softly from behind a palm bush where the hen, Eggy, was in great trouble.

Eggy was in the habit of escaping through a hole in her hen coup and she always laid her eggs in all the funny places around the colony. And just then, she was sitting on her three eggs in the rain and a tapping sound was coming from one of them. Eggy was wet but she did not want to move and Spotty, the kind hearted pup, was giving her company and protection.

"Tap Tap!" came the sound of little beak working inside the egg-shell. The children all tiptoed and gathered around the hen.

"Tap Tap!" and they all became silent to hear the sound,

Tap! And . . . . then there appeared a crack in the center of the egg and a small white head with a yellow beak came out. It was followed by a pair of legs and a fluffy ball of body.

"A chick!" the children shouted in amazement.

"Woooof!" said Spotty.

"Cluck" "Cluck" cried the proud hen and put the chick under her wings; it was Eggy's the very first chick.

The children erected a small shed over Eggy with leaves and paper and left her to take rest. They came back then to finish the game. Rusha continued to take her turn. She said, she wanted to be a pilot and she flew her plane fast.

Tim wanted to be an actor and little Ninni wanted to be a sailor.

It was little Joe's turn in the end. He decided that what he really wanted was, to be a dog like Spotty, who saved Eggy and its eggs in need. So Joe ran around on all his fours and barked on all the children against the backdrop of candle and he sat near Spotty then to learn more.

It was hilarious but not good and no one laughed at his actions. No one explained him anything but Joe felt ashamed of himself. His elder sister Rusha realized that he was too small to know, what he wanted to be, and she said,

"Joe, you need to be a good person first."

The shadow game ended with fun. And now when anyone asks little Joe what he wants to be when he grows old, he has an answer,

"I want to be a good person first."

26

Light, sound and action

Trisha leapt from her bed and rushed to get ready.

Everyone knows how hard it is to get up when you have gone to bed late the night before. You have all your sweetest dreams in the morning, especially if you have to go to school. Trisha was watching TV till 12 pm and now—she was behind time.

Trisha entered her class breathlessly and she heard Rita Ma'am announcing a surprise test. She sighed, "First I am late and now this surprise test!"

It was a bad day for Trisha again. She lost out on many things and all because she was late. She was punished for being un—attentive and she was ridiculed for her unmatched pair of socks. She came back home with a heavy heart. She picked up her mother's mobile and started texting sad messages to her dad and other friends,

"Another unlucky day for me," she wrote.

And ah . . . ha, her spirit soared high as she started getting replies immediately,

"Oh!"

"How sad."

"Hey, what happened?" She then forgot all about the bad day and started messaging her friends joyously. Her colony friends, playing in the park, were one less. And little Raghu was sent to call Trisha to join them.

Three, is no company,

We are short of one.

The game we want to play,

Only four is fun.

When Trisha saw Raghu at her door, she said quickly,

"Hey, I am busy, I am texting."

"Oh, why should you text, I thought you could always speak on mobile." Raghu was surprised.

And little Trisha took a long time explaining the fun involved in sending and receiving the short messages.

"Please Trisha, come and play one game with us then text the whole world about it," Raghu pleaded. And Trisha agreed unwillingly.

The four friends played 'Football' for a long time. What fun they had! Little Trisha was at her best. She ran as hard and kicked as many goals as she could. It was a perfect evening and her cheeks were red in the cold air. The streams of frosted air were coming out of her mouth. And when it was time to go home, Trisha was as hungry as a wolf.

Trisha was free early that night. With a game of Football with her friends, she was full of energy. She had finished her homework, put her bag and changed her clothes too. She was happy but she was not sleepy. Though she had promised her mother to sleep early the same day, but she went to her to take permission to watch television.

"Come and sit with me," mom told her, "you are going to read a lovely story from this book full of pictures."

"Mom, cartoons are also stories," Trisha argued.

"But with reading you think, you imagine and you use your brain where as TV gives light, sound, colour and action effect all together. You feel good but sleep is far," mother explained.

"Reading? . . . err . . . ok!"

Little Trisha could hardly understand what her mother said but one thing was sure, within fifteen minutes of reading she fell off to sleep.

And so it was that every evening, Trisha sat with her mother before bed time and read a story from the big colourful book and each morning she did get up in time.

27

Strange taste

"Peter, eat your sandwich."

"Paul, drink your milk."

That was what the twin's mother was always telling them. And the two did not like that at all. Peter and Paul were very fond of eating pastries and cookies with soft drink which their mother of course, never gave.

One summer afternoon, when the parents were away for shopping, Peter sneaked into the kitchen after lunch. He wanted to drink something sweet but there was nothing in there. Paul was thirsty too and he joined him in his search. The twins searched the whole kitchen up and down and their search ended inside a big cupboard in a corner.

The two naughty children were always poking their nose into things that their mom said not to. And the wooden cupboard was one such thing that was always kept closed. The children opened the cupboard and found it full of different pots, containers, bottles and jars of all shapes and sizes. Peter shouted happily,

"Mommy is out shopping,

We are but by our self!

Our favorite many drinks are,

All here, on this shelf!!"

Out of so many of bottles, one strange bottle caught the children's attention the most. It was a shiny transparent little bottle full of gold and chocolaty liquid. It seemed to be full of melted chocolate and Peter took a quick small sip from it.

Uh . . . . ! Eh . . . . !! It had a strange taste.

"Oh, it is not good," he told Paul, "you won't like it."

"But I like anything that is sweet, is it not sweet?" Paul inquired.

"Errr . . . . well, it is sweet but I bet you can't take more than a very small sip," Peter replied sincerely.

"Of course, I can!" Paul was sure.

And the two brothers placed the bet that if Paul drank even half the glass of that strange drink, Peter would give him his full pocket money of that month.

Curiosity kills the cat. Little Paul took one small sip from it and felt peculiar.

"It is not all that bad," he mumbled and gulped down half of the glass of it without giving a second thought. The stake was high, little Paul wanted to win the bet money.

And Ahem . . . ! Paul felt as if he had swallowed a whole bunch of spiky cactus down his throat. His mouth was on fire. He coughed and coughed and lunged for breath. Something was wrong with him definitely.

"Is he going to die?" he feared.

He screamed loudly holding his neck, "Ooh, my mouth, ... ooh!"

"Granny . . . . granddad, come quickly. Paul has hurt himself," Peter called loudly.

Though granddad and grand mum came running but they did not understand as to what would have happened. Little Paul was feeling choked.

"He is looking terribly sick," grandpa said.

"Call the doctor," granny shouted. But Mala, the house maid could guess, "There was a Vodka bottle kept in the cupboard and it looks that Paul has taken that," said she.

The experienced aunty gave him a sandwich to eat then. Little Paul munched the sandwich and mumbled,

"Alcohol is really bad for health."

Paul did not remember anything after that as he slept all the day long. And the next morning when he got up, he still had that strange taste in his mouth.

Paul and Peter never poked their nose in an unknown territory ever. Now whenever they see any one taking alcohol they say,

"Don't drink that awful stuff, you will fall sick."

They never bet on money also. Mom had, of course, stopped their pocket money for a year.

28

Best painting

*T*eacher's Day was coming soon. Ria's mother gave Ria some money to buy a gift for her teacher but Ria chose to make a card herself.

Ria was a pretty red-haired girl who was also very strange. She was never happy and contended with her own things and preferred what was not hers. She liked her friend's toys, her cousin's clothes, her parent's books and so on. And very strangely, she often wished, if she had another girl for her sister but not Maira.

Ria was six and her big sister Maira was sixteen. And little Ria hated her sister being so much older than her and it was all because she could never play dolls and hop-scotch with her. Maira would always say,

"I am too old for these games."

And Maira's maturity stood in between their bonding.

All through the evenings, in and out of their colony, Maira and her friends practiced a music band, cycled to exercise, went to theatres and spent lot of fun time together and they always took Ria along. But little Ria did not appreciate that. She would pout, scowl and march off always in huff for any flimsy reasons. She did not like Maira having so many good friends and enjoying so much.

Ria with her sister always fell out,

We friends wonder, what is it all about?

Maira is good, Maira is caring,

And for that Ria could not agree,"

Maria's friend laughed and sang when they played their band and Ria would be angrier than before.

One day before the 'Teacher's Day' little Ria sat down with a paper and her paint box to make a card for her loving teacher. She painted on the card an autumn scene, with its yellow and red trees. She decorated the trees with artificial dry flowers. The card was beautiful and Maira approved and admired it sincerely,

"This is your best painting yet," she said. But suddenly, Maira's friends barged into Ria's room and took them by surprise.

"Here we are!" they shouted together.

And, oho, the paint brush slipped from Ria's tiny hand and her pretty picture was ruined completely, "Oh, we are sorry!" said the friends.

But Ria was pale as lily.

Seeing her little sister's tears, big sister simply had to help. She took the paint brush and went to work on Ria's spoiled picture. Her friends then went to the kitchen and found some seeds of different shapes and colours. Maira painted some leaves on the card and made them red and brown. And her friends added a pile of burning leaves with different seeds at a corner. The flames were of different colours—yellow, blue, red and even green.

It was a pretty picture with a theme 'Not to burn Green'

"That's wonderful!" exclaimed a happy Ria.

Maira, Ria and all the friends then played hide and seek in the garden.

They also took turns on the swing and when the sun went down, the friends went home but not before giving a 'We are Sorry' card to little Ria.

"What luck to have a big sister after all," said Ria and ran to make one more card for her lovely sister, her teacher at home.

29

The car accident

"A Get well card for Tanav," said Vishv.

"Oh dear," said Tanav's mother, taking the card, "he's not well and he is sleeping."

Tanav was so unwell that he spent most of his time in bed. He had been ill for the past few months. He was suffering with fever and headache. Though the doctors had given him many medicines, antibiotics and injections . . . but they were of no help, the high temperature had showed no signs of coming down.

Every morning, little Vishv came to see his friend and a fine friendship they had but Tanav hadn't any strength left to play or talk. The car accident that he escaped narrowly had traumatized his young mind for ever.

It was a terrible accident on the city-highway a few months back. Tanav's auto-van had missed the 'head on' collision with a truck by chance but the drunken truck driver had crushed another car with Tanav's friend in it. Tanav had been frightened and nervy ever since. He was now spending his days meeting different doctors and the terrible nightmares won't allow him to sleep at night.

Tanav missed his friends, his teachers and his school and he had lost most of his second term in school. He had nothing much to do in his lonely room except to look out of his window and see the stars, the moth, the bees and the birds—but he was safe at least. And so he thought. He would often cry hiding his face,

"What a pity—I am not a part of the bright world outside."

Tanav was unhappy and a feeling of despair grew in him gradually until one fine day he noticed a peculiar site outside his window. A monkey—fat and tall, appeared in his balcony and was eating a cheese burger. He had covered his head *with a red stole and was holding a mirror. He was looking into it and was making funny faces at his reflection.*

Tanav found it very funny. He called up his mother, but as he called, the animal disappeared from there, leaving the half eaten burger on his window sill.

The next day, Tanav found a pink Kungfu panda on his balcony at the same time.

The fat panda was wearing a yellow diaper and was flying a blue kite. Tanav laughed at his jolly antic and lo, when he was having so much of fun, the huge animal disappeared leaving his kite and thread behind.

Once Tanav saw a 'Batman' taking milk from a feeding bottle and the other day there was a 'Spiderman' playing hop scotch with a red ball. These events were so silly and hilarious that little boy could not help himself enjoying and they left him always in splits.

Tanav was mystified and he did not dare to tell it to anyone.

Of course no one would believe.

But thankfully bit by bit, his temperature went down, his headache vanished and boredom went too. He slept well and often dreamt about the Panda in the diapers and the Spiderman with lollypops. His health improved and the day came soon when he started going back to school again.

In the school, the first day itself, he shared the secret of the magical cartoon characters visiting him during his illness to his best friend Vishv and . . . ,

Ahem!

There was another secret waiting for him in his class room's cupboard.

Some fancy dress suits of tiger, monkey, spider man and batman were kept there neatly—Ms. William, his great teacher wanted to entertain Tanav somehow and put humor in his otherwise tragic life.

The daily doses of laughter put the joy back in his mind and body. And his friends could do what the medicines could not.

30

A quiet evening

*A*ll the family members were sitting comfortably around a sparkling fire lit in the living hall. Winters had arrived. Granny was knitting a pair of red woolen socks, mother was talking to her two daughters, Chumky and Pinky and dad was reading an old news paper.

Tu-whit! Tu!

"*Tu-whoo,*" spoke a wet grey spotted owl and sat on the dry window sill near the fire. It was injured and had lost its way in the rain. And it was also looking for the warmth. The girls crowded around the little owl to keep it warm and mother gave him some fresh water to drink. Dad quickly cleaned his wound and granny brought some rice and dried seeds for it to peck.

And suddenly, by mistake, Pinky disturbed Chumky's milk mug and the milk got spilled a bit on the floor. Chumky was most annoyed by this and she pulled Pinky's pony tail then in anger.

Pinky, who did not like this at all, ran near her mother and got entangled in the granny's wool and tripped.

And when mother tried to help Pinky, she herself slipped over the milk on the floor.

Dad tried to give a helping hand to both mother and Pinky and lo, his news paper flew and landed on the bone fire.

"*Oh! What a commotion it was!*"

Paper!!

Pinky!!

Wool!!

Fire!!

And for a while, all the family members were shouting, helping, protecting and running after each other in a complete chaos. The grey owl and granny became a referee and started whistling and shouting together,

"Tuhu!"

"Don't run!"

"Tuhu!"

"Hold on!"

Hearing that, they all stopped and started laughing together. It was of course, a silly thing to happen on a cold rainy day. And then the breeze grew colder and stronger and mother became restless all the more.

'I don't like winter,' declared she, with a shiver.

"It's so chilly and children catch awful colds and flu. Ooh, it's a bad weather."

"But mom, I love winters. We should have been in a big mall now, shopping and eating, if only, it was not raining," Pinky said.

"And what fun it would have been to play with the friends in this cold weather," sighed Chumky.

"Don't be silly!" father said, "winter or summer, it is lovely to be home with the family in a quiet evening like this."

Dad was comfortable in his armchair now with a hot cup of coffee.

"That's good, at least someone is happy staying home with me," said granny softly.

"*Granny, we are happy too,*" *shouted Chumky and Pinky together,* "*and mom, we too want a hot cup of coffee.*"

Mom brought hot coffee with crème for everyone and some more seeds for the owl. The owl tweaked,

> **"*Tu-whit Tu, Tu-whoo,***
>
> **For the nuts, thank you!**
>
> **Family is happy, Evening is quiet,**
>
> **I am full and I am dry!!"**

He flew up on to the head of a fan and perched for the night. And the girls realized that it is simply a matter of being able to see the good side of things.

31

Bread crumbs

Rihan was watching his favorite show on TV. He was comfortable and warm under his blanket when mother Ashima suggested him to visit their next door neighbors, Mr. and Mrs. Ghosh to socialize.

"Rihan, Mr. Ghosh loves playing chess with you on a Sunday and Aunty has made lots of cookies, just for you."

"Good, I would love visiting them too," cried Rihan, jumping to go.

"But mom, our one neighbor does not want to be disturbed and being visited ever. He lives all alone in the far end of the colony and keeps his doors and windows shut," Rihan told his mother.

"Here, take some good books for him too, I think, he needs your friendship and a little care," mother Ashima said.

Rihan and his friends worked hard to befriend the lonely neighbor and called him 'Lonely uncle'.

Uncle lonely had no name plate on his house and his letter box remained always empty. It was left open carelessly throughout the day. One day to make him happy, children put some fresh flowers and a best wishes card there. The children wondered what lonely uncle would say the next day. But to their surprise, uncle never checked their gift and the flowers died and became very dark and dry. A white and a grey pigeon made a nest on those nice dried stalks of dead flowers and laid two eggs.

Mr. Alone heard the pigeons cooing from his letter box some days later, he was thrilled, "Oh, I am so lucky," he cried, "these pigeons have chosen my letter box to lay the eggs!"

The children's gift then became really precious to him. He started taking care of the bird family and threw bread crumbs to them daily. One cloudy morning Rihan noticed that there were no crumbs for the birds on the ground, "Perhaps uncle has not woken up yet."

He went to his house and called him up but there was no answer. And when he went inside the house to check, he found a sick uncle on his bed, without any food and medicine.

"Birds need crumb, it is noon,

Oh, my friends, please, come soon!

Get some help, and be so quick,

Uncle lonely, has fallen sick."

Rihan called his friends again and again.

The children knew their responsibilities well. Debby brought some hot soup, Kittoo brought some bread and curry and Raima brought some fresh apples for the un-well neighbour. And little Ansh brought some crumbs for the hungry birds too.

With so much of love and attention, uncle was better soon. He thanked the children sincerely with a small party. And one day to Rihan's surprise, he appeared at his door and declared,

"I am Uncle Raj and I have come here to socialize."

Rihan looked at his mother and they both smiled and said,

"Welcome!"

INFORMATION ABOUT THE AUTHOR
AND HER PREVIOUS WORK

*M*s *Seema Johri, granddaughter of late Shri Bhagwati Charan Varma, Padam Bhushan and an eminent Hindi writer, has done her graduation from I.T.College Lucknow and post-graduation from Lucknow University in Sociology with first class first.*

She is a teacher by heart and spirit and has spent more than 15 years as a teacher in various schools of high repute.

She has a deep love for children and sincerely believes that children are like fresh clay and they can be moulded into any form by their parents. She also believes that the parents must define a bench mark set of Indian values and enforce them in the daily lives of their children to cultivate a desired national character. With such benchmarks, when these children become the next generation, the community and country would be more humane.

Her first book "The Security Umbrella" is about vigilant parenting. Some of our Indian kids have become directionless and are posing a threat to the dignity of our society. The ever increasing crime, greed, dissatisfaction, lust and anger in their culture indicate degradation of moral and social values in them. Indian parents though work hard and provide the best to their children but forget to equip them with values that automatically bring out the best in them.

Our country runs on some core values and in spite of so many ups and downs, it has survived because of these values only. The values are the protocol for decent and desirable behavior for our collective survival and collective progress, they are our roots and our children need the firm roots to grow and humane dreams to fly.

The book, The Security Umbrella provides a guideline to develop these core Indian values, a kind of moral armament, in the children during their formative years by their parents. The vigilant parenting can never spoil a child's life, but a lack of it always breaks a parent's heart and a country's dream.

The book is now on line, with Lulu Publishers and can be read on www/Lulu.com or seemajohri.com